Story Time with Signs & Rhymes

There's a Story in My Head
Sign Language for Body Parts

by Dawn Babb Prochovnic
illustrated by Stephanie Bauer

Content Consultant:
Lora Heller, MS, MT-BC, LCAT
and Founding Director of Baby Fingers LLC

magic Wagon

visit us at www.abdopublishing.com

For Stephanie Bauer, who magically illustrates the stories in my head—DP
For Lottie and Marleanne, two mischievous monkeys!—SB

Published by Magic Wagon, a division of the ABDO Group, PO Box 398166, Minneapolis, Minnesota 55439.

Looking Glass Library™ is a trademark and logo of Magic Wagon.

Printed in the United States of America, North Mankato, Minnesota.
102011
012012
 This book contains at least 10% recycled materials.

Written by Dawn Babb Prochovnic
Illustrations by Stephanie Bauer
Edited by Stephanie Hedlund and Rochelle Baltzer
Cover and interior layout and design by Neil Klinepier

Story Time with Signs & Rhymes provides an introduction to ASL vocabulary through stories that are written and structured in English. ASL is a separate language with its own structure. Just as there are personal and regional variations in spoken and written languages, there are similar variations in sign language.

Library of Congress Cataloging-in-Publication Data

Prochovnic, Dawn Babb.
  There's a story in my head : sign language for body parts / by Dawn Babb Prochovnic ; illustrated by Stephanie Bauer.
    p. cm. -- (Story time with signs & rhymes)
  Summary: Playful images and simple rhymes introduce the American Sign Language signs for different parts of the human body.
  ISBN 978-1-61641-842-7
  1. Human body--Juvenile fiction. 2. American Sign Language--Juvenile fiction. 3. Stories in rhyme. [1. Human body--Fiction. 2. Sign language. 3. Stories in rhyme.] I. Bauer, Stephanie, ill. II. Title. III. Title: There is a story in my head. IV. Series: Story time with signs & rhymes.
  PZ10.4.P76Th 2012
  [E]--dc23
                          2011027077

Alphabet Handshapes

American Sign Language (ASL) is a visual language that uses handshapes, movements, and facial expressions. Sometimes people spell English words by making the handshape for each letter in the word they want to sign. This is called fingerspelling. The pictures below show the handshapes for each letter in the manual alphabet.

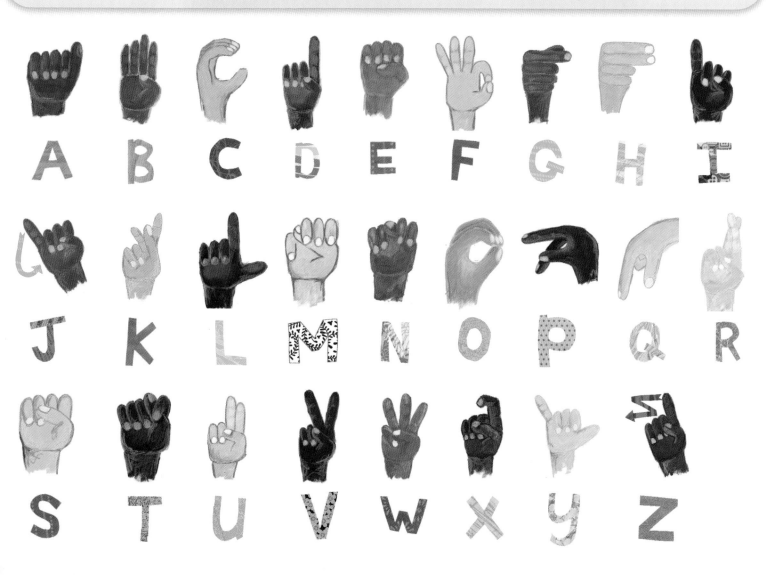

There's a story in my ears. I can hear it when you giggle.

ear

There's a story on my **lips.** I can feel it in a kiss.

lips

There's a story in my **toes**. I'll sit back and let them wiggle.
Imagine all the stories I can write!

toes

9

There's a story on my **tongue**. I can taste it when I'm eating.

tongue

There's a story in my **eyes**. I can view it through a lens.

eye

There's a story in my **heart**. Listen closely to it beating.
Imagine all the stories I can write!

heart

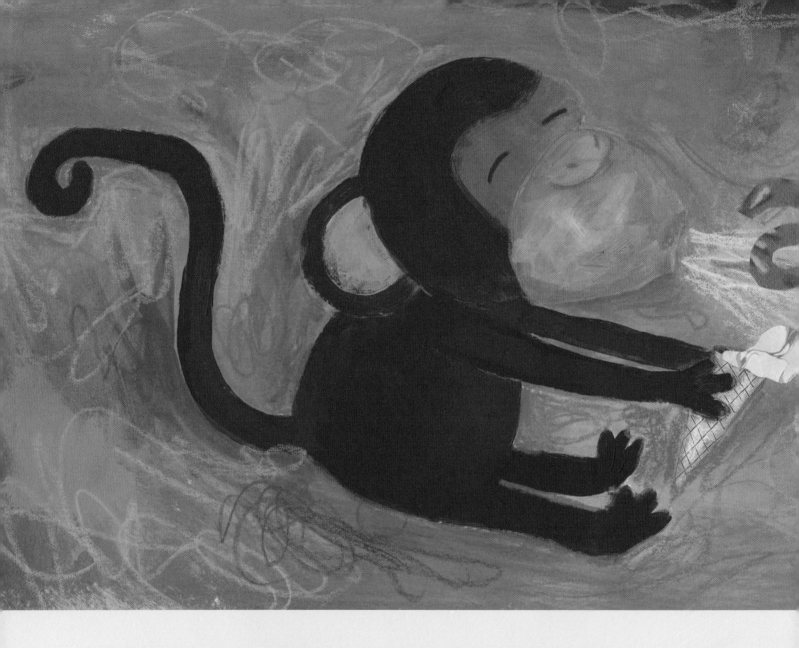

There's a story in my **nose**. It blows through me when I'm sneezy.

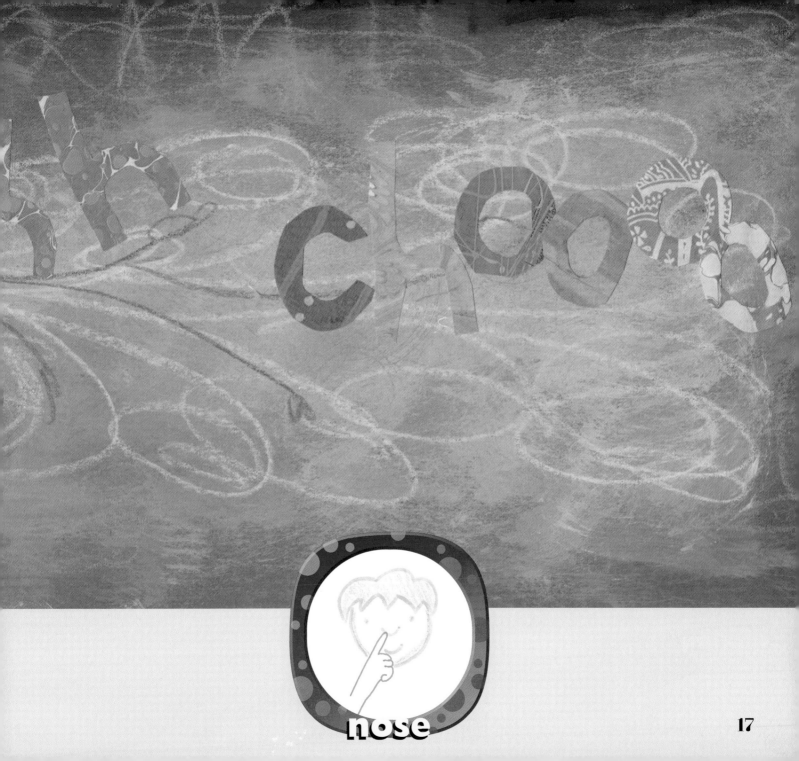

nose

There's a story on my **face**. It appears when I'm upset.

face

There's a story in my **arms**. Rock the baby, nice and easy.
Imagine all the stories I can write!

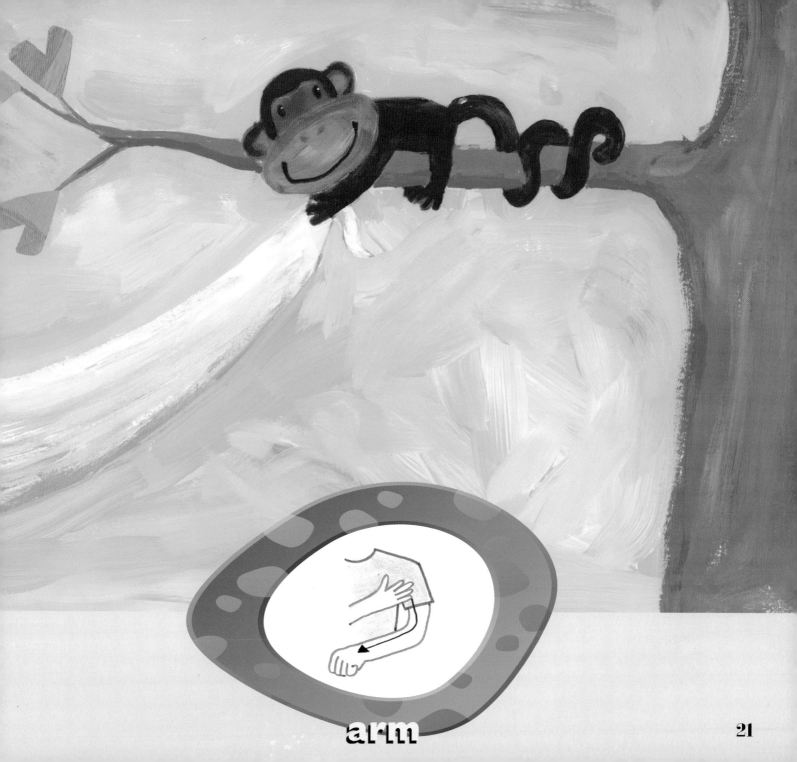

arm

There's a story in my **head**. I can see it when I'm napping.

head

There's a story in my **lungs**. It escapes with every song.

lungs

There's a story in my **hands**. Celebrate! My friends are clapping!
Get busy! There are stories YOU must write!

hand

American Sign Language Glossary

arm: Hold your left arm in front of your body with your palm facing down and your elbow bent. Now slide the palm of your right hand across the back of your left arm, starting near your left armpit and moving toward your wrist.

ear: Pinch your earlobe between your thumb and pointer finger and wiggle it a bit. You can also just point to your ear.

eye: Point to your eye. If you are talking about both eyes, point to both eyes. Some people point to their eye with a double movement, like they are tapping their eye.

face: Use your pointer finger to draw an imaginary circle around your face.

hand: Hold both hands with your palms facing you. Rest one hand on the palm of the other, then move it down diagonally as if you are drying it off on a towel. Repeat this motion with the other hand if you want to say *hands*.

head: Bend your fingers at the large knuckle and touch your fingertips to your temple and then to the side of your chin. Your palm should be facing down. It should look like you are showing the location of your head.

heart: Tap your heart two times with the middle finger of your "Five Hand." Your heart is on the left side of your chest.

lips: Use your pointer finger to draw an imaginary line around your lips.

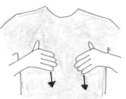

lungs: Bend your fingers at the large knuckle and touch your fingertips to the top of your chest. Now slide your fingertips down to the middle of your chest. Repeat this a couple of times. It should look like you are showing the location of your lungs.

nose: Use the tip of your pointer finger to tap the tip your nose a couple of times. Some people just point to their nose.

toes: Hold your hands in front of you with your palms facing down and your fingers pointing toward your toes. Now wiggle your fingers just like you might wiggle your toes. Another option is to simply point to your toes with your pointer finger.

tongue: Open your mouth and use your pointer finger to tap near your tongue a couple of times. You don't actually need to touch your tongue!

Fun Facts about ASL

In ASL, to talk about a body part, you often just point to it. If you're not sure of a sign for a word, you can always fingerspell it, even if there is an ASL sign for that word. When you fingerspell, you make the handshape for each letter in the English word you want to sign.

Most sign language dictionaries describe how a sign looks for a right-handed signer. If you are left-handed, you would modify the instructions so the signs feel more comfortable to you. For example, to sign *arm*, a left-handed signer would slide the palm of the left "B Hand" across the back of the right arm.

Just as there are personal and regional differences in spoken and written languages, there are similar variations in sign language. If you want to learn more about sign language, ask a parent or teacher to help you meet someone from the Deaf community. This is a great way to learn the most current and correct signs in your area, and you might even make a new friend!

Signing Activities

Body Art: This is a fun activity for partners. Get some blank sheets of paper and some markers. Take turns being the artist and the signer. The first artist draws a picture of one part of the body listed in the glossary. The signer must make the sign for that part of the body. Switch roles until all the parts of the body listed in the glossary have been drawn and signed at least once.

Copy Cats: This is a fun game for a classroom or group of friends to play together. Players sit in a circle and choose one person to be the leader. All players close their eyes while the leader counts to three. On the count of three, each player makes the sign for one part of the body as they open their eyes. Any player who makes the same sign as another player must move out of the circle, and the game continues with the remaining players. If all the remaining players make the same sign on a turn, the turn does not count. The last player who remains in the circle wins and becomes the next leader. If two players remain at the end, a tiebreaker round is played. In the tiebreaker round, the players and the leader do a sign for a body part each time the leader counts to three. The first player to make the same sign as the leader is out, and the remaining player is the next leader.

Additional Resources

Further Reading

Coleman, Rachel. *Once Upon a Time* (Signing Time DVD, Series 2, Volume 11). Two Little Hands Productions, 2008.

Edge, Nellie. *ABC Phonics: Sing, Sign, and Read!* Northlight Communications, 2010.

Heller, Lora. *Sign Language for Kids*. Sterling, 2004.

Valli, Clayton. *The Gallaudet Dictionary of American Sign Language*. Gallaudet University Press, 2005.

Web Sites

To learn more about ASL, visit ABDO Group online at **www.abdopublishing.com**. Web sites about ASL are featured on our Book Links page. These links are routinely monitored and updated to provide the most current information available.